1

Explore to Learn More!

- **Historic Bonnet House Museum and Gardens**
  - o 900 N. Birch Road, Fort Lauderdale, FL 33304
  - o (954) 563-5393
  - o https://www.bonnethouse.org

- **History Fort Lauderdale**
  - o 231 SW 2nd Ave, Fort Lauderdale, FL 33301
  - o (954) 463-4431
  - o https://www.historyfortlauderdale.org

- **Naval Air Station Museum Fort Lauderdale**
  - o 4000 W Perimeter Rd, Fort Lauderdale, FL 33315
  - o (954) 359-4400
  - o https://www.nasflmuseum.com/

- **Stranahan House**
  - o 335 SE 6th Ave, Fort Lauderdale, FL 33301-2256
  - o (954) 524-4736
  - o https://stranahanhouse.org/

Mitchell's Mysterious Day in the Bermuda Triangle

by
Bill Sydnor

Photographic Credit:

Historic photographs in this publication, unless otherwise noted, are the property of **the Fort Lauderdale Historical Society and the Naval Air Museum/Fort Lauderdale** and are reproduced here with their permission.

Special Thanks:

To the memory of Minerva Bloom for her dedication to education and preservation of our unique history–and to the Naval Air Station/FTL Museum.

Please Note:

A percentage of the proceeds from the sale of this book
will be used to assist historic preservation efforts in south Florida.

For additional information, visit
Mitchell's Magical Days on Facebook

Mitchell's Mysterious Day in the Bermuda Triangle

Table of Contents

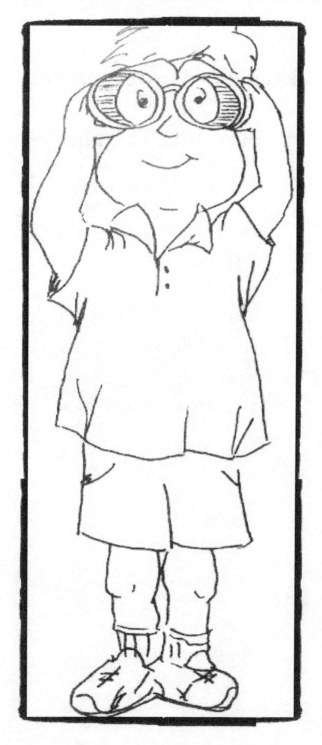

1.

WHAT TRIANGLE?

"Come on, Mitchell, get up. Time to get going," Pop Pop whispered as he nudged Mitch's shoulder while he slept. "Time's a'wastin'." Mitch pulled the blanket up over himself and buried his head under his pillow.

"Five more minutes," he muttered.

"No, boy, we've got to get going. Those fish aren't going to wait."

"Well, I think they can wait five more minutes," Mitch moaned.

Pop Pop loved fishing. He fished from boats, he fished from piers, he fished from seawalls, he fished from the beach. His old car was filled with fishing rods and tackle boxes and the trunk smelled like a bait shop. The cats in the neighborhood loved it and gathered together to spend their nights in the tattered back seat.

"Come on, let's go," Pop Pop insisted as he tickled Mitch's foot under the blanket.

"Okay, okay!" Mitch sat up in his bed and tried to focus his eyes. "Oh, Pop Pop, come on...it's still dark out!" he exclaimed.

"Shhhhh. You'll wake your mother."

Mitch dragged himself to his closet and grabbed an old t–shirt and some shorts. "Why do fish want to eat so early?" he muttered as he searched for his sneakers.

Pop Pop and Mitch unloaded the fishing gear from the car and made their way to the water's edge. The ocean was flat and calm. Stars danced in the sky as the moon watched off to one side. A sliver of sunlight peered over the horizon. Palm trees stood motionless, as if they were sound asleep. Mitch thought he should be asleep, too.

Pop Pop opened a folding chair and sat down with a "plop." It sank deep into the sand. He began fiddling with the line at the tip of his fishing rod, attaching bits and pieces of stuff from his tackle box.

"Bluefish are running with the incoming tide," he explained as he reached into the cooler for bait. "And the sun's comin' up. They'll bite on squid and shiners this time of mornin'. Here, watch me." He laid a squid atop the silvery shiner, pinched them together tightly between his thumb and finger and hooked them together. His hands worked skillfully and quickly. "Line 'em up, side by side. Make sure they're set good. Then give 'em a hoist." He slowly brought the rod back over his right shoulder and snapped it like a whip. The bait soared in an arch over the water and splashed down fifty feet away.

Pop Pop handed Mitch a squid. "Your turn." The pink, slimy squid slid between Mitch's fingers and landed in the sand. Mitch stared at it blankly.

"Oh, um…I think I'll wait for you to get the first bite."

Mitch loved spending time with Pop Pop, but he didn't share Pop Pop's enthusiasm for fishing. He was more interested in what was happening on the water.

"Okay, okay," Pop Pop chuckled. "I guess I'm the only 'Old Man and the Sea' out here today!" He was referring to a very famous book by author Ernest Hemmingway about a fisherman who never gave up.

Mitch sat near the surf, gazing out to the ocean. "Can't see a thing. Just darkness," he sighed. "At least the sun still gets to sleep."

"Hey, Mitchell! I almost forgot. I brought something for you." Pop Pop reached into a cooler.

"Yeah! Squid and shiners!" Mitch laughed.

Hey, Mitchell! I almost forgot. I brought something for you."

"No, no. Wait a minute. Wrong place!" he laughed. "Here, take my rod. Try to keep the bait moving." Pop Pop wiped his hands on an old towel, then rummaged around in a deep canvas bag. "Here they are." He handed Mitch a worn leather case with a thin strap and metal clasp.

"Go ahead, look at what's inside." Mitch opened the case and took out a pair of old binoculars. They were heavy, painted black with dull brass showing through in some places.

"I've had these since I was a boy," Pop Pop said. "My father gave them to me." Mitch handed the fishing rod back to Pop Pop and held the binoculars to his eyes. He looked out toward the horizon. "If you look carefully, very carefully, you might see things other folks can't see." Pop Pop continued.

While Mitch adjusted the binoculars, Pop Pop reeled in his line. The bait was gone; there was nothing left on the hook. "Thieves," Pop Pop muttered. "These Bluefish are clever. Think you can steal my bait, do you?" He grabbed another squid and a shiner.

"Hey, Pop Pop, isn't there a shipwreck around here somewhere?" Mitch asked as he wiggled his toes in the wet sand.

"Lots of 'em, boy. This ocean's littered with wrecks. Many ships foundered here. Some have never been found. Claimed by storms, reefs, attacks…and the triangle!"

"What triangle?" Mitch's ears perked up. "Ships sank in a triangle?"

Pop Pop took his eyes off his line for a moment and turned to Mitch. "Well, there's not really a tri –" Suddenly, something pulled at his line. Pszzz –pszzzz, went the fishing reel. Pszzzzzzz….

"I got something here!" Pop Pop yelled as he cranked the handle on the fishing reel. "I'm gonna get 'em! These Bluefish put up quite a fight, but I'll get 'em!" His rod twitched and yanked back and forth as he struggled to bring in the line. "I'll teach you to steal my bait! Hey, Mitch, Mitch!" he called. "Grab the net and follow me!" Pop Pop began walking into the surf and he continued his fight. Mitch was lost in his imagination. "A triangle in the ocean…"

"Mitch!" Pop Pop called again. "I need your help. Come on! Quick, Mitchell, grab the…" And just like that, it was too late. The rod straightened and relaxed, the fighting stopped, the fish had broken free and escaped. "Hmmph," Pop Pop sighed. "Coulda been our dinner." He stood in the surf and looked at Mitch. "Hey, did you hear me? I said that could have been our dinner."

Mitch still wasn't paying attention. Pop Pop placed the fishing rod into a holder he had stuck the sand. "Mitch, you missed the whole thing. I had something on the line there. A Bluefish, I'm sure of it. Didn't you see?" Mitch just sat in the sand, staring out toward the horizon. "Uh…hello, Mitch? Are you somewhere out in space?"

Mitch looked up at Pop Pop. "Wha–What?" he replied. "Am I what?" He paused for a moment and asked, "Hey Pop Pop, where's that triangle? I've been looking, I don't see it."

11

Pop Pop chuckled. "Well, it's not like there's a triangle painted out there on the water." He reached into his bait bucket and grabbed another squid and shiner. With the skill of a pro, he twisted them together onto his hook. "It's really a region…an area of the Atlantic Ocean in the shape of a triangle." He gave the bait a tug to make sure it was secure. "An area where lots of strange things have happened." Pop Pop whipped the rod from back to front and sent the squid and shiner sailing out over the ocean. Kerplunk! "Lots of strange things that no one can explain. Like the story of the Cyclops."

"A cyclops?!" Mitch exclaimed, thinking of a mythical one–eyed monster.

"The U.S.S. Cyclops. A Navy ship. She disappeared out there somewhere about a century ago. Not a trace of her…or of her crew or her passengers. Not a single trace…"

"The ship just disappeared?" Mitch asked.

"Seems to have," Pop Pop continued. "Some folks thought she was sunk by German submarines. Others thought her heavy cargo shifted in a storm and caused her to capsize. The strangest theory was that a giant squid had risen up from the sea, grabbed her with its tentacles, and dragged her to the bottom."

"Giant squid!?" he exclaimed. He looked into the bucket of bait squid and tried to imagine them as giant, huge slimy, pink monsters.

"Never a trace of her or her men...." Pop Pop sat in his chair and waited for a bite.

"There's a triangle in the water where strange things happen?" Mitch chirped. "And giant squid attack ships?! A Cyclops ship?" He held Pop Pop's binoculars to his eyes and scanned the ocean. There wasn't much to see. The sun was lazily climbing over the horizon. A half dozen pelicans glided overhead in v–formation, searching for a fishy breakfast. On the beach, sandpipers, gulls, and terns pecked at seaweed and sand for whatever they could find.

Mitch kept looking through the binoculars. Far in the distance, south by southeast, a ship sat in the stillness. There wasn't enough light to make out what kind it was. He adjusted the focus wheel to get a better look.

Mitchell held Pop Pop's binoculars to his eyes and scanned the ocean.

"I see something, Pop Pop, but I can't make it out."

"What's that, Mitch?" Pop Pop asked as he adjusted his line. "What'd you say?"

The image started to grow fuzzy. Mitch rotated the focus wheel from one side to the other, hoping to get a clearer view, but the focus just got worse. "What's happening?" Mitch wondered. "Why can't I see clearly, Pop Pop?"

Suddenly, he felt a firm hand on his shoulder.

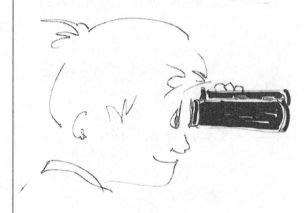

2.

CYCLOPS!

"What are you doing here?" spoke a stern, deep voice. "Are you a stowaway? A stowaway! How'd you scramble aboard? Were you hiding in the shipping crates back in Barbados?"

Mitch looked around him, expecting to see Pop Pop. Instead, he found himself squatting under a dirty, wet canvas tarpaulin on the deck of a huge ship.

"I–I was..." he stammered. "I was fishing. And then, I– we were... I mean, I was looking.... with my Pop Pop."

The African–American man cut him off. "You looking for a trip? An adventure at sea? That there's the truth, isn't it, son? You ran off and thought you'd like a trip on this old ship...a trip to a new land. A new life. Did you know we're headed to Baltimore? Or maybe you don't care where we sail. Just wanted a life at sea."

"I–I…I had no…. I mean, I was fishing with my Pop Pop and then was looking through his…"

"A lot of my people seek work aboard these ships. But what about you, then? Did your Pop Pop put you aboard to become a man? My father did the same. I had to seek my opportunity at sea."

"No, I…I mean yes, I my Pop –, but I…" Mitch stuttered as a large wave crashed onto the foredeck and flowed like a river to the stern of the ship.

"Stand up, son. Let's have look at you."

Mitch pushed the tarpaulin aside and stood.

"You smell of fish!" the dark man laughed. "You're young for a seaman. How old are you, son?"

"I'm ten," Mitch replied.

"Well, I wasn't much older than you when I set out to sea. You'll learn, you'll learn fast. You'll have to aboard this hull."

"Who…who are…? Where am…are…? Mitch asked as another large wave broke over the side. He nearly lost his footing.

"Brace yourself!" the man instructed as he brushed the salt water from his face. "I'll be your charge while you're aboard. I'm Fireman Third Class Earl Whitehall," he said as he steadied Mitch. "What's your name, son?"

"Mitchell. I'm Mitchell Allen Andrews." Mitch shook Earl's hand. "Or just Mitch. Mostly just Mitch." He looked down the length of the ship. It seemed to be ten football fields long. "Where are we?" he asked.

16

"Well, Mitch, I think we're now about 1500 miles from Baltimore. We have a long way yet to go. We're runnin' this old hull on only one engine, so our progress is slow. Painfully slow. It's already March 4*th*, well into 1918, and we're far behind schedule."

"1918?!" Mitch yelped.

"Right! We should be off the coast of Virginia by now, but this old girl's crippled. Barely crawling through these seas. Oh, she was a strong ship in her day, the Cyclops was. She was launched back in 1910 to help with war efforts. Now she's being used to refuel and refit other ships…and to carry cargo. That's what we're doing this run. Carrying a full cargo."

Mitch sat motionless. "The Cyclops?" he thought to himself. "The Cyclops!"

"We've had more than our share of trouble this trip. We were only a few days out of Brazil when Cyclops lost her starboard engine. Cracked a cylinder. Commander Worley had no choice but to shut that engine

down. Now, with only one engine, we barely make 10 knots at full speed, and we've lost our ability to outmaneuver German U–boats."

"U–boats?" Mitch stammered.

"Submarines. With this war, the Germans could have U–boats in these waters and with only one engine we're a sitting duck, a huge target for their torpedoes. We weren't expecting to stop in Barbados. We were scheduled for a clear run from Brazil up to Baltimore harbor. But Commander wanted to take on more supplies, so we made port in Barbados."

Earl continued. "What's more, this ship is heavily loaded, carrying 11,000 tons of manganese ore in her holds, so she sits deep in the water. Too deep. The sea breaks over her decks. Her maximum capacity is 8,000 long tons...so we're overloaded. Commander Worley really can't expect us to make Baltimore on schedule at this rate. A heavily loaded ship with a bad engine that's running at less than 10 knots and can barely be steered. And all of her officers locked in the brig...."

Mitch had stopped listening. He quivered with fear as Pop Pop's words ran through his mind: "The Cyclops...not a trace of her...no trace of her crew ...not a single clue..."

"We have to do something! We have to!" He panted, as if he were about to faint. "Turn it around. Turn the ship around. It's not too late, right? We can make it back to land if we turn around. Where's the...? Go tell the captain!"

"What? Commander Worley? Go tell Commander Worley to turn Cyclops around?! You have a sense of humor, you do. Worley's our biggest problem. Before we reached Barbados, the officers were talking. They said Worley had gone mad. They said he was no longer fit to be in command of the Cyclops, so they wanted to mutiny." Earl looked into the distance.

"Yes, a mutiny, like what happened aboard Bounty. Have you heard of the Bounty? There was mutiny of her crew." He looked into Mitch's eyes. "This crew aboard Cyclops was willing to risk their lives...risk being hanged to keep this ship safe. But they're right. Commander Worley has gone mad. He has! Day after day, he walks the length of these decks, barking out orders, waving a cane...sometimes in full dress uniform, other times he's wearing only a derby hat...and his underwear!"

Mitch giggled under his breath.

19

"No, no, no, son– that's nothing to laugh about. Nothing at all! He's lost his mind." Earl adjusted his cap. "So, Worley caught wind of the crew's plans to take away his control. To take the helm of Cyclops. He flew into a rage, ordered the crew to seize all the officers and lock them up below decks. Oh, it was a bloody struggle! In the middle of it, Worley drew his pistol and fired. He shot one of his own officers and had the body tossed overboard."

"He wh–what? He shot a man?!" Mitch chirped as he started to crawl back under the canvas tarp.

"Shot him dead. That's what I was told. Sent him to the depths." Earl explained. "Just imagine what he could do to me, a dark–skinned man?" Mitch scooted deep under the tarpaulin.

Captain Worley

20

"That's probably a good idea, son. We can't let Commander Worley see you. He won't take well to a goldbricking stowaway. He might toss you into the drink."

"But Earl... this ship...the Cyclops! It's going to–I mean, we have to..." Mitch insisted.

Earl cut him off mid–sentence. "Just stay here, out of sight." He glanced at his pocket watch. "I have to go, I'm due for my inspection rounds. I'll come back as soon as I can. I'll try to bring you some food from the galley." Earl walked hurriedly down the long deck and, when he was nearly out of sight, he turned back and gave a slight wave to Mitch.

U.S.S. Cyclops

U.S.S. Cyclops parts box taken off the ship before her final voyage.

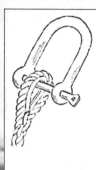

3.

NAVAL AIR STATION FORT LAUDERDALE
NASFL

"What are you doing down there, Mitch?" Pop Pop asked as he pulled back the corner of his beach blanket. Underneath, Mitch was curled up tightly. "I know you don't like early morning' fishing, but the sun's up now! Come on, it's time for us to head home. Fish don't bite after sunrise." The bright sunlight stung Mitch's eyes for a minute. He struggled to get his focus.

"Commander Worley?!" he gasped. "I, uh... I...." His heart pounded inside his chest.

"Come on, boy. Help me gather up this stuff."

"Yes, y–y–yes, C–c–commander," Mitch stuttered as he sat on the sand, the blanket still clinched in his fist. "I was just...Earl told me to..."

Pop Pop folded his chair, tucked his rod under his arm and grabbed his bait bucket. "Earl?"

Mitch rubbed his eyes and looked up at Pop Pop. "Yeah...right. Earl. He could be in trouble." He let out a weak sigh as he gazed toward the horizon, searching for the Cyclops.

Pop Pop wasn't listening. "I'm not too happy going home empty handed," he grumbled. "We have no fish; we've got no more bait. Time to call it quits. Grab the tackle box, will you?" He motioned to Mitch. "And fold up the blanket." Mitch kept rubbing his eyes. The blanket–or was it the tarpaulin aboard the Cyclops?

"Did you get sand in your eyes? You keep rubbing them." Pop Pop asked.

"No, I was just… I thought I…I saw…."

"Well, come on, then. Let's get going." Pop Pop helped Mitch fold the tattered blanket. "Hey, are you hungry? How about some breakfast?"

"Food!" Mitch thought aloud. "That's right! Earl was going to bring me some food." He looked puzzled.

"Earl? Who's this Earl? One of your buddies?" Pop Pop asked. "Well, if your friend Earl was bringing us food, he never showed up and I'm not waiting around. Let's head over to the pier restaurant." He placed his hand on Mitch's shoulder, then stopped and gave it a sniff. "Hmm. You smell a bit ripe. Folks'll think we're having eggs, toast– and smelly squid!" he snorted as he made his way through the soft sand.

Mitch followed a few steps behind. He took one last look over his shoulder hoping to spot the Cyclops. There was no sign of her. He gave a slight wave to Earl.

On the pier was a small restaurant with a few booths outside and tables and chairs inside.

"Outside it is. Always outside unless it's raining." Pop Pop inched himself into a wooden booth and sat with a solid 'thud.' Mitch sat across from him facing the ocean and placed the binoculars on the table.

"Pop Pop," he asked, as pelicans floated by on the breeze, "whatever happened to the Cyclops? Where did she go?"

Pop Pop was dunking a piece of toast into his dark coffee. Crumbs floated on the surface. "No one knows." He took a munch, then a slurp and dabbed his moustache with his napkin. "I guess you'll have to ask the triangle. It holds secrets."

"What kind of secrets?"

"Well, Mitch, all kinds. Some folks think the Cyclops was swallowed up in a giant whirlpool and pulled down to the depths of the ocean."

"Wow!" Mitch exclaimed.

"You see," Pop Pop explained as he finished off his toast, "there are sinkholes in parts of the Atlantic Ocean, some not far from the shoreline of Florida, like Red Snapper Sink. A huge underwater sinkhole."

"Is that in the triangle, Pop Pop? Is Red Snapper Sink in the Bermuda Triangle? Is that where the Cyclops wound up?" Mitch asked excitedly.

"No, no. Red Snapper Sink isn't in the triangle, it's north, near Saint Augustine, but it might explain why some odd things occurred. These sinkholes on the bottom of the ocean are deep holes on the ocean floor, shaped like a funnel. There are legends that these holes can create huge whirlpools on the ocean's surface, putting ships at risk."

"I get it! Like a whirlpool in the bathtub!" Mitch chirped. "So, maybe it was a whirlpool that sank the Cyclops. Maybe she sank because of a hole in the floor of the ocean…at Red Snapper Sink, like the drain in the bathtub!"

"Well, that's one of the theories. Of course, no one knows if any whirlpool from a sinkhole would be powerful enough to pull in a big ship like Cyclops. And it's unlikely that Cyclops was in the area of Red Snapper Hole when she disappeared, but it's one of the theories. Lots of theories about what happened to her."

Pop Pop lowered his coffee mug. "This stuff really interests you, doesn't it, Mitch? I tell you what, let's make a trip down to the Naval Air Museum. They have history a great deal of history about the triangle that'll grab you!"

"That's great! Can Billy come, too? And Austin?" Mitch chirped. Austin was Mitchell's fuzzy terrier dog.

"Sure, sure. Billy is welcome to join us…but I think Austin should

 sit this one out," Pop Pop said as he popped the last piece of soggy toast into his mouth.

The Naval Air Station Museum sat at the far northern side of a road that wound all around the Fort Lauderdale International Airport. In front of the museum was an Avenger torpedo and a submarine torpedo from World War II. and an AA (anti–aircraft) gun from World War I. Mitch and Billy ran ahead of Pop Pop for a closer look.

26

"P–choo, p–choo!" Mitch sounded off as he looked up the site of the AA gun. "P–choo!"

"What is this place?" Billy asked.

"Well," Pop Pop explained, "this is a museum that has preserved the history of our local Naval Air Station and helps us remember all the men & women who trained here to defend our country during World War II."

"You mean, soldiers trained here? At this airport?" Billy continued.

"Yes, well…not exactly. There were Navy Airmen that trained here, and the airport looked nothing like this back in the early 1940s. We're here so Mitchell can learn more about the Bermuda Triangle." Pop

Pop reached over and tousled Mitch's hair. The three of them walked up the wide wooden steps and entered the museum. Right away, a model of an aircraft carrier caught Billy's attention.

"Look! Look over there! I want that!" he exclaimed. A gentleman came up behind him.

"I'm afraid that's not for sale," he chuckled. "It's here to stay as part of our museum collection. My name is Tim and I'm a guide here at the Naval Air Station, Fort Lauderdale. Have any of you been here before?" he asked.

"I have," Pop Pop replied. "A few times. But this is the first trip for Mitch and his friend, Billy."

"Welcome!" Tim offered. "I'll show you around. Here at the Naval Air Station Museum, we have artifacts that relate to the history of the Naval base which was located here during World War II."

"Was the Cyclops near here?" Mitch asked. "The Cyclops was a Navy ship. It disappeared in the triangle."

"Oh, you know about the Bermuda Triangle, do you?" Tim asked. "Well, no, the U.S.S Cyclops was not a part of the Naval Air Station. The Cyclops was a vessel during WWI."

"She disappeared! There was a mutiny by the crew, or maybe she got sucked into a whirlpool." Mitch said excitedly. Pop Pop patted Mitch on the shoulder.

"My grandson is very intrigued by the Bermuda Triangle. I brought him here because I know this museum has it's own Bermuda Triangle mystery, one that has never been solved."

"That's right!" Tim chirped. "One of the most famous mysteries of the Bermuda Triangle originates from right here."

"What?" Billy gasped. "Something disaapeared here?"

"In December 1945, five Navy planes on a training mission left the Naval Air Station in Fort Lauderdale. Less than 2 hours after takeoff, the flight commander reported that he couldn't get his bearings. None of the planes was ever found."

"Never seen again?!" Billy gasped.

"That's right," Tim stated. "In fact, the last location they provided was about 50 miles south of here, give or take, and maybe a couple hundred miles offshore." He motioned toward the southeast. "They were over the Atlantic. It was very stormy that day. Bad storms that quickly got worse. He walked toward a mural on the museum wall. Billy was talking with Pop Pop, but Mitch had other things on his mind.

"Five planes. Fifty miles south. Over the Atlantice ocean...." Mitch said to himself.

4.

FLIGHT 19 IS LOST.
I REPEAT, FT-28 IS OFF COURSE.

Mitch took Pop Pop's binoculars out of their leather case, wandered into a small room in the museum and peered out the window. "I wonder..." he said to himself as he held the binoculars to his eyes. The view was blurred and he struggled to get it into focus. Outside was a small parking area surrounded by trees. Mitch focused into the distance to a clearing next to an airport runway. "Ah, nothing," he mutterered under his breath. He scanned to the north and south, at ground level.

Slowly, the scene in the binoculars changed. An airfield came into focus, lined with large, silver planes.

"What's this?" Mitch turned to ask Tim, but no one was around. He found himself inside a far different room with men in uniforms scrambling to answer a call over a large radio.

"Cannot see land," a voice said. "We seem to be off course."

"What's our compass reading?"

"I don't know where we are. We must have got lost after that last turn."

"Hey, listen to this!" came a call from an airman in the radio room. "I think it's Flight 19...FT–28, it sounds like Lieutenant Taylor."

Suddenly, another voice came over the radio. "This is FT–74, Lieutenant Robert Cox, plane or boat? Calling 'Powers' – please identify yourself so someone can help you."

There was no answer, but Mitch could hear background conversation from the radio's speaker. An airman in the room stated, "That's Cox, his crew is flying maneuvers Just offshore."

Lt. Cox tried again to reach Flight 19 from his plane, "This is FT–74, what is your trouble? Calling FT–28, Lieutenant Taylor, this is FT–74, what's your trouble?"

A man responded, "We cannot be sure where we are. Repeat: cannot see land. Both of my compasses are out, and I am trying to find Fort Lauderdale, Florida. I am over land, but it's broken. I am sure I'm in the Keys, but I don't know how far down, and I don't know how to get to Fort Lauderdale."

"We can't find west," the man continues. "Everything is wrong. We can't be sure of any direction. Everything looks strange, even the ocean," called an unknown member of the flight crew.

Lt. Cox spoke again, "NAS Fort Lauderdale, this is FT–74. Report. Flight 19 is lost. I repeat, FT–28 is off course. FT–28 reports their location is somewhere over the Keys." He Paused a moment, then called for Lt Taylor. "FT–74 calling FT–28. Taylor...put the sun on your port wing if you are in the Keys and fly up the coast until you get to Miami. Fort Lauderdale is 20 miles further, your first port after Miami. The air station is directly on your left from the port."

Taylor responded: "We are heading 030 degrees for 45 minutes, then we will fly north to make sure we are not over the Gulf of Mexico."

"What is your present altitude? I will fly south and meet you," Lt. Cox instructed.

Taylor answered, "we have Just passed over a small island. We have no other land in sight... can you have Miami or somewhere turn on their radar gear and pick us up? We were out on a navigation hop and – I thought they were going wrong, so I took over and was flying them back to the right position. But I'm sure, now, that neither one of my compasses is working."

"Your transmissions are fading. Something is wrong. What is your altitude?"

Mitch watched unnoticed in a corner of the room. He stood totally still and silent. Additional officers raced into the room. One barked, "What're their bearings?"

"I'm at 4,500 feet. One of the planes in the flight thinks if we went 270 degrees, we could hit land. We are heading 030 degrees for 45 minutes, then we will fly north to make sure we are not over the Gulf of Mexico," Taylor's voice replied.

"Tell Taylor, FT–28, to switch radio frequency," ordered a naval airman at the base. "There may be interference. Tell him to go to the search and rescue frequency,"

Taylor replied, "I cannot switch frequencies. I must keep my planes intact."

A different pilot's voice came through the radio. "Dammit, if we could Just fly west, we would get home; head west, dammit."

Taylor then added "We'll fly 270 degrees west until landfall or running out of gas."

Mitch slid down the wall and sat on the floor. The office became tense, the men in uniform were talking, one after the other. "We've triangulated their position. They're within a 100 nautical mile radius of 29°N 79°W. That puts them north of the Bahamas and well off the coast of Daytona, Florida."

Taylor's voice cut in from his plane, "Holding 270. We didn't fly far enough east; we may as well just turn around and fly east again".

"What? What in the world are they doing? The weather out there is deteriorating fast!"

Taylor's voice crackled over the speaker. "All planes close up tight ... we'll have to ditch unless landfall ... when the first plane drops below 10 gallons, we all go down together....we'll ditch together."

A new voice transmitted to the tower, but it was trembling, bordering on hysteria. "We can't tell where we are... everything is... can't make out anything. We think we may be about 225 miles northeast of base..." For a few moments, the pilot rambled incoherently before uttering the last words ever heard from Flight 19. "It looks like we are entering white water... We're completely lost."

The radio went silent. "I think we've lost contact," reported a radioman in the room.

"What was their last heading?"

"...It seems like they're flying east, toward the open ocean. I think they're about 200 miles offshore....visibility is approximately 800 to 1200 feet, estimated wind, west southwest about 25 to 30 knots. The air is turbulent, the sea is rough."

"Keep trying!"

"Calling FT–28. Come in FT–28."

Eerie silence.

"This is NASFL base calling FT–28. Respond. This is NASFL base calling FT–28. Respond. FT–28...Lt. Taylor, can you read us? Come in...."

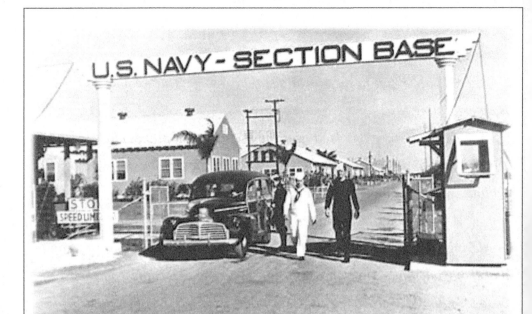

U.S. NAVY - SECTION BASE

PORT EVERGLADES
FT. LAUDERDALE, FLA.

Marshall Ordered Planes To Hawaii

FORT LAUDERDALE DAILY NEWS

IN EVENING EDITION

FORT LAUDERDALE, FLORIDA, THURSDAY, DECEMBER 6, 1945

FOURTEEN NAS AIRMEN MISSING

Pearl Harbor Inquiry

Fighter Aircraft Sent To Islands

GM-Union Wage Issue Parley Set

Stalled Car Sank Five Germans, Col.

Cold Wave Postponed For County

Search Launched For Lost Planes

Hurley Claims Acheson Hurt Iran Policies

Hotel Project Would Relieve Labor Housing

Speaker Flays Homestead Act On Exemptions

Planes Attributed Afraid To Guess

Rent Overcharges Here Hit $1,213

Senators Scrap Over Wage Bill

Surplus Property Probe Advocated

House Speeds Curb On Labor

Gen. Short Warned Of Surprise Raid

Jap Politicians Ordered Arrested

Captain Ordered Ship Abandoned

Traffic Arrest Held Unlawful

Ship Hits Mine; Crew Missing

Col. Broward Ships

Units Of Navy, Army, Coast Guard Scour Sea For Lost NAS Aircraft

Broward County 'E' Bond Sales Lag As Victory Loan Drive Nears End

Lieutenant Charles Taylor
Flight 19 Leader: FT–28

Lieutenant Robert F. Cox
Flight Instructor 19/Pilot: FT–74

Lt. Commander Don Poole USN
Flight Training Officer in the
control tower communicating
with Flight 19.

NAS Fort Lauderdale
Control Tower 1945

38

MOUNT CARMEL ITEM

FIVE NAVY BOMBERS VANISH

BEHIND THE HEADLINES

Gen. Marshall Tells Of Attempt To Build Up Hawaii's Defense

BULLETINS

Searching Plane With 12 Aboard Dives In Flames

BY RICHARD C. GLASS

MIAMI, Fla. Dec 6 (UP) — A Navy Patrol Bomber carrying perhaps 12 men crashed in flames into the Atlantic last night while searching for five Torpedo Bombers which it disappeared mysteriously, it was revealed today.

Committees Appointed By Grossman

Two Kulpmont Residents Held Without Bail

HURLEY CHARGES POLICY IN IRAN WRECKED BY ACHESON

DAILY NEWS

FINAL EDITION

TWO SECTIONS — FIVE CENTS

THURSDAY, DECEMBER 6, 1945

Navy Planes, 28 Aboard, [H]unted Off Florida Coast

5 Lauderdale Avengers, Rescue Bomber Missing; Carrier Joins Search

By MILT SOSIN
(Miami Daily News Staff Writer)

Six navy planes with 28 men aboard were missing off the Florida east coast today as navy, coast guard and army air and surface craft, including an escort-aircraft carrier, joined in one of the most widespread searches.

Apparently a victim of the same sea which swallowed up five TBM Avenger torpedo bombers and their crews totaling 14 men last night, a huge navy seaplane bomber — a Martin Mariner — which had joined the search, was reported overdue by the commandant of the Banana River naval air station and itself became the object of another search.

A merchant vessel reported seeing flames flare 100 feet into the air off Ponce de Leon inlet, near Daytona Beach, last night, but no wreckage was found this morning. An oil slick was reported in the area, but authorities at Banana River said there was no evidence that this came from the Mariner.

Hundreds of planes and surface craft flew low over the ocean off Miami, Hollywood, Fort Lauderdale and Palm Beach and other east coast cities as they combed an area far out to sea in which the five torpedo bombers were believed lost.

BABY FLAT TOP OF THIS CLASS IN SEARCH
The St. Lo, Sister Ship of the Escort-Carrier Solomons

Example of U.S. Navy Master Radio
Station Receiver Room, 1945

40

5.

Then What Happened?

"Here you are! We've been looking all over this place for you." Pop Pop extended his hand to Mitch and helped him get on his feet. "What are you doing sitting in this old room all alone?"

Mitch rubbed his eyes. "I'm not all alone, Pop Pop. I'm listening to the airmen talking with Lt. Taylor. He's lost!" Mitch looked around him. He and Pop Pop were the only ones there. "But I–I heard them. I did, right here!" Mitch grasped the binoculars. "Unless…"

"What you might have heard was Tim explaining what happened to Flight 19. There were five Avengers that left here for a training mission and never returned. Did you fall asleep in here? You look a little confused."

"Yeah, that was it! Flight 19. FT–24 was calling FT–29 and they lost contact. Then their radios went silent. Where are they?"

Pop Pop looked into Mitchell's eyes. "No one knows. After more than 70 years, what happened to them remains a mystery."

Tim walked into the room. "That's right. It's still one the great mysteries of the Bermuda Triangle."

"What do you think happened, Tim?" Pop Pop asked.

"Well, there are lots of theories about what happened to the planes. Some think that Lt. Taylor flew into an electromagnetic disturbance that caused his compass to malfunction. It's thought that Taylor went far off

41

course after his compass gave him incorrect information. From the transcripts of radio transmissions, Taylor thought he and his squadron were over the Keys. He brought the planes into a northeast heading, which he felt would lead them all back to the air station."

"Yeah!" Mitch yelped. "He thought he was over the Gulf of Mexico. FT–74 told him to keep the land over his port wing and go up the coast."

"What's a port wing?" Billy asked.

"His left wing. We refer to left as port and right as starboard," Tim answered.

"Just like on my boat, Mitch," Pop Pop added.

"You seem to have read up on this," Tim said to Mitch. "You even know the pilot's call numbers!"

Mitch held Pop Pop's binoculars and stammered. "I–I uh, like… I did read it. Or maybe I got if from the Internet or something."

Tim continued. "We think Taylor led the Squadron far out into the Atlantic, where they encountered stormy weather. The planes banked toward the Florida coastline…and all radio transmission was lost."

"They ditched! They ran out of fuel. Lt Taylor said they would all do it together." Mitch chirped.

Tim replied, "the Navy's Board of Investigation Report on the loss of Flight 19 states that an aircraft carrier, the USS. Solomons, picked up a radar signal off the coast of Daytona Beach from four to six unidentified planes. The signal put them over North Florida, about 20 miles northwest of Flagler Beach."

Mitch, Pop Pop and Billy listened carefully as Tim continued.

"Two of the planes were flown by Navy crews, three were flown by Marine crews. When they became lost, the planes may have scattered. It's possible that the three Marine planes flew toward the Gulf of Mexico while the two Navy planes flew south."

"Then what happened?" Billy asked.

"Well, based on their last know position and the radio call, it appears that they all ran out of fuel . . .and crashed."

"I remember, years back, when a wrecked Avenger was discovered in the Everglades. As I recall, they were pretty certain it was from Flight 19," Pop Pop stated.

"Wow," yelped Mitch. "Which one was it? Was it Lt. Taylor's? Can we go see it?"

Tim explained. "Yes, there was wreckage spotted by a helicopter pilot in the Everglades back in 1989. The wreck was found 36 miles inland from the Atlantic Ocean, just 20 miles away from the Naval Air Station."

"That close?" Pop Pop sighed under his breath.

"Photos of the cockpit were taken, and it was determined that the plane was a TBM Avenger–3, the same type of plane flown by Lt. Charles Taylor."

"They found Lt. Taylor's plane? Can we go see it?! Please?" Mitch pleaded to Pop Pop.

"Well, I'm afraid not," Tim countered. "Several experts studied the photos taken of the wreck and realized the plane was not part of Flight 19. The crash site was too far away from their last known position, which was over the ocean, somewhere 150 miles east of Daytona Beach."

Tim continued, "But other experts disagreed. A rubber heel found at the wreckage site came from a size 11 or 12 shoe, a close match to Lt. Taylor's. And the Navy had no record of a TBM–3 Avenger missing anywhere in Florida between 1944 and 1952, except for Charles Taylor's plane. Finally in 2014 the Navy identified the Avenger wreckage, and it revealed it was not one of the planes from Flight 19."

Mitch and Billy were paying close attention.

"Let's go see it!" Billy squealed.

Tim began to explain, "Apparently, once word got out that one of the missing planes from Flight 19 may have been found, hunters, air boaters, and people who knew the Everglades wanted to see it for themselves. They may have taken pieces of the wreckage for souvenirs because now no one is able to find any remains of that Avenger.

"So, it disappeared, too…." Mitch muttered under his breath.

Flight 19 Crew

TMB Avenger Instrument Panel

45

Example of TBM Avenger Bomber Flight Crew: Pilot, Gunner, Radioman

6.

GOTTA GET OFF THE COTOPAXI!

When Mitchell and Billy got home, they were still very excited and more curious than ever about the Bermuda Triangle.

"Whataya wanna do now?" Billy asked.

"Let's ride bikes." Mitch replied.

"Where to?"

"The beach."

"The beach? That's kinda far" Billy sighed.

"Come on!" Mitch dashed to the carport and grabbed his bicycle. Billy did the same.

"Wait, wait!" Pop Pop called.

"Uh–oh," Billy moaned.

"Where are you two off to?"

"Whataya wanna do now?"

Mitch answered slowly. "Umm, we might ride... you know, to the beach."

"Oh, I knew you were up to something." Pop Pop laughed.

"I want to see the Bermuda Triangle. Can you see it from the beach?" Mitch asked.

"Funny thing is – yes you can. You can't really see a triangle out there, but those waters are part of the Bermuda Triangle! Just offshore."

"Wow! Billy exclaimed.

"Hold on, wait a second," Pop Pop called as he walked back into the house. A few minutes later, he returned with the black case with the long leather strap.

"Your binoculars!" Mitch chirped.

"Yeah, I think we should take these with us."

"Are you going with us?" Billy asked. "Do you have a bike?"

Pop Pop paused. "No, no. We'll take my car. I'm a little worried about you boys riding that far on your bicycles this late in the day."

Mitch and Billy parked their bikes in the carport and climbed into Pop Pop's old car.

"Just move the fishing rods out of the way." Pop Pop moved a tackle box from the back seat and a cat leapt out an open door.

The beach was just a short drive from Pop Pop's house. The warm air felt good as it raced through the car's open windows. Mitch took Pop Pop's binoculars from the old leather case. "I wonder what we'll see," he thought, as he shifted the focus knob back and forth. Pop Pop parked at the edge of the sand and the boys jumped out.

"Come on, Mitch!" Billy nudged Mitchell with his elbow. "I'll race you to the water."

The sun hung lazily to the west. On the beach, sandpipers, gulls, and terns pecked at seaweed and sand for whatever they could find.

Mitch wasn't paying any attention to Billy; he was already looking through the binoculars. Far in the distance, past a line of condominiums and houses, a dozen sailboat masts stood proudly toward the clouds. He adjusted the focus wheel and scanned out toward the ocean.

"Hey Billy, I think I see something, but I can't make it out." The image started to grow fuzzy. The shoreline disappeared into a fog of storm clouds. Mitch rotated the focus wheel left and right, hoping to get a clearer view. "Billy, I..." Suddenly everything changed. Mitch felt a hand land firmly on his shoulder.

"What are you doing here?" spoke a stern, deep voice. "Are you a stowaway? A stowaway! How'd you scramble aboard? Did you sneak on while we loaded in Charleston harbor?"

"I–I was..." Mitchell stammered. "I'm here with my friend. And my Pop Pop. I– we were... I mean, I was looking...." Mitch answered nervously as he searched for Billy.

The man cut him off. "Handle that line."

"I–I...wha –?...." Mitchell clutched the binoculars. "What, do you mean–who...?"

"Handle the line! We're headed into a blow. Hurry! Ah, lad, you act like you've never handled a line."

Mitch stared straight ahead. He was aboard a ship that was at least a few football fields long. "What–wh–where am I?" he asked. "Oh, no! Is this the Cyclops again?" He looked at the binoculars that hung from his neck. "Did these put me back aboard the Cyclops?!"

"No son. You're aboard the S.S. Cotopaxi. Did you get confused in port? Did you climb aboard the wrong vessel?"

Mitch stood frozen. "Cotopaxi? What is that? Where are we?"

"Well, I estimate we're about 200 nautical miles south of Charleston," the stranger explained. "At this point, we have another 300 to go before we make port in Havana. We're five days into the trip, but a strong gale caught us off guard. Might have to change course."

50

"Havana?" Mitch yelped. He tried to look through Pop Pop's binoculars, but the sea spray had coated the lenses. "I was, uh–I was I was searching just searching for the triangle and I... the Cotopaxi?"

"Yep, the ol' Cotopaxi. Have you heard that she's a cursed ship? It could be so." Mitch listened while he wiped the binocular's lenses with his shirt. The man continued. "From the time her keel was laid in 1918, seems she was destined for hardship. Her first year, she ran aground off the coast of Brazil and was badly damaged. One of her engines needed repair and her prop strut and rudder were ripped from under her. Nearly sank. Five years ago, in 1920, she collided with a tug in Charleston harbor. Dragged that tug all the way to the bottom!

"Yep, some say she's cursed from the start." The man leaned on the rusty railing and gazed out past the waves. "My father always said that any vessel involved in collision at sea carries a curse 'til her end. So, what's your name, son?"

"Mitch. Mitchell Allen Andrews, sir."

"How old are you, Mitchell?"

"I'm ten, sir," Mitch replied.

"Well, Mitchell, I'm Able Seaman Charles McFarland." Charles extended his hand to Mitch as a wave broke against the hull. Mitch struggle to stand. Mitch's mind wandered. "I remember! I've heard about the Cotopaxi." He began to quiver with fear. "The Cotopaxi...she disappeared in the Triangle a long time ago! It was never seen again. Not a trace of her or her crew...not a trace." His heart raced, "We have to get

51

off this thing! The Cotopaxi is in trouble...we're in trouble! How can we get off before..."

S.S. Cotopaxi

"Get off? What, boy, get into lifeboats in this sea? What are you prattling on about? It's just fear. Fear's gotten a hold of you..." Charles *looked into the distance. "Try to calm yourself."*

Mitch held the binoculars to his eyes, looking for the beach, hoping to see Pop Pop. "I gotta get off the Cotopaxi before it disappears in the triangle..."

"Ah, I think I scared you with this talk of a curse on this old ship. You're so young to be at sea, son. Fear is always with us. It's part of our life." Charles knelt next to Mitch. "Son, the Cotopaxi's hull is tired. She's got a belly full of coal and a gale is in our path." Charles scanned the

horizon. *"Captain discovered that our ship was riding below the Plimsoll line."*

"Below the Pumsaw...?" Mitch asked softly.

"The Plimsoll line. It's a mark painted on her hull to show how deeps she sits in the water. Cotopaxi is overloaded. Captain made a stop in Barbados for inspections. They found no leaks, no problems, so don't worry, son, we'll will make it to Havana without issue..."

"But Charles...this ship...the Cotopaxi! It's going to–" Mitch yelled. Charles cut him off mid–sentence.

"Hey, now! Give me a hand with these hatches. They're taking on water, they're in quite bad shape. Shoulda been repaired before we left port, but we were given orders to sail on to Cuba. Now we're facing a gale...winds up to 60 knots. Oh, this is going to be a long night."

A wave taller than the side of the ship slammed the Cotopaxi. Charles fell onto the deck near a metal railing, got up and hurriedly made his way to secure a metal hatch.

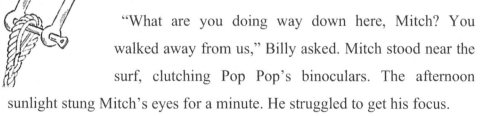

"What are you doing way down here, Mitch? You walked away from us," Billy asked. Mitch stood near the surf, clutching Pop Pop's binoculars. The afternoon sunlight stung Mitch's eyes for a minute. He struggled to get his focus.

"Where's Charles?" he gasped. "I, uh... he fell..."

53

Mitch stood near the surf.

"Come on, Mitch. It's time to go. We're all heading back home."
Mitch sat rubbing his eyes. "What were you doing, anyway?" Billy asked.

"No, I was just… I thought I…I saw….is he okay?"

"Is who okay?"

"Charles… is Charles okay? Where is the ship?" Mitch spoke
quietly.

"Oh, come on," Billy interjected, "let's get going. You're acting
kinda weird. I think you're imagining things! Maybe you got dizzy." Billy
led Mitch up the beach toward Pop Pop's car. Mitch took one last look
over his shoulder hoping to see the Cotopaxi. –There was no sign of her.

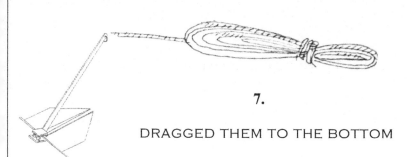

7.

DRAGGED THEM TO THE BOTTOM

"Pass your homework forward. Make sure your name is on it, otherwise I won't know it's yours." Mrs. Jennings stood before the desks as the students rummaged in their bookbags.

"Mrs. Jennings, may I ask you a question?" Mitch asked as he held up his hand. Mrs. Jennings continued gathering the homework.

"Yes, Mitchell."

"Have you ever heard of the Bermuda Triangle?"

"Oh, sure I have," Mrs. Jennings answered. "There have been many books, even a few movies, about that area of the Atlantic Ocean."

"My Pop Pop took Billy and me to the Naval Air Museum this weekend. Five navy airplanes disappeared from there. And ships disappeared to–the Cyclops…."

"Yes," she replied, "They never found those five planes. And the Cyclops! That's a great mystery!"

Rachel chimed in. She never, ever raised her hand. "Why did they disappear, Mrs. Jennings?"

"I read that sailors believed giant squid would rise from the sea, grab the ships with their tentacles, and dragged them to the bottom." Jerry added. The entire class gasped.

"There aren't really sea monsters, right? She's just kidding us," many students asked, talking over one another.

Mrs. Jennings took the laptop off her desk. "Let's take a look." Her fingers danced on the keyboard. "Oh! Look at this!" She began to read aloud. "Saint Augustine. November 1896. 23 feet long, 18 feet wide, multiple legs, with silvery–pink skin 3 ½ inches thick. Look!" She showed the class an image on the screen.

"Wow!" everyone exclaimed.

Mrs. Jennings continued reading. "The head has the shape of a sea lion's head. The mouth is protected by two tentacles 8 inches in diameter, 30 feet long, resembling giant elephant trunks. An additional tentacle extends from the head and two others from each side of the head 15 feet."

"Ick, gross!" Rachel squealed.

"The tail is jagged with cutting points and has two more 30–foot tentacles. The eyes are under the back of the mouth."

Yvonne made a gagging sound.

"It took 6 horses to move it near the railroad to be studied," Mrs. Jennings continued. "It is considered to be an example of a giant squid. Sailors in the old days thought they were some kind of sea monster that pulled ships to the bottom of the ocean."

"Well, if that's what's out there, I'm never going swimming in the ocean again!" Yvonne smirked as she shook her head.

"Old time sailors thought sea monsters grabbed ships," Jerry repeated. "But we know they didn't. Right?"

"Yeah!" Inson agreed. "There's no such thing as sea monsters that sink ships."

"Well, as I . . ." Mrs. Jennings began. She was quickly interrupted by Rachel.

"Okay, right. So, how do you explain this thing?" she asked as she pointed excitedly at the pictures of the squid.

"Rachel, Jerry, class, let me finish. Yes, for many centuries, sailors could not explain mysteries that surrounded them at sea. And some of those mysteries were blamed on very odd, giant sea creatures that were thought to cause ships to simply vanish without a trace."

Mrs. Jennings's fingers tapped on the laptop until she found what she was searching for. She held up another image for the class to see. "Like this!" she added.

"That sea monster sure looks like the sea monster that washed up on the beach!" Yvonne barked.

"Yes, it does," Mrs. Jennings explained. "This drawing depicts a giant squid. It says here there are no real accounts of any giant squid attacking a ship anywhere at any time. Actually, giant squid sightings are extremely rare because they live in very deep water."

"This one made it to the beach!" Rachel chirped.

"Well, yes it did," Mrs. Jennings answered. "From these old images, it looks like he got pretty beaten up along the way. Scientists think it was attacked by a school of sharks, then it washed up here."

Mrs. Jennings continued her explanation. "Sailors off Florida's coast faced many challenges, but scientists know that giant sea monsters wasn't one of them." She laughed lightly. "There were plenty of obstacles to deal with... sudden storms, strong currents, and of course–pirates!"

"AArrgh!" Billy growled. The kids all laughed.

"Oh, we had plenty of pirates here!" Mrs. Jennings chimed in. "Pirates from all over the world came to Florida, like Sir Francis Drake, Captain Kidd, Jennings, and Blackbeard– "

"Jennings?!" Jerry exclaimed. "Whaaa–?"

"Mrs. Jennings, you're related to pirates?" Billy asked.

"Well, I–I, uh, I don't know. I don't think so," she stammered. "Maybe we can find out."

Yvonne giggled. "Our teacher is a pirate! Aaargh!" The class broke into laughter.

"Mrs. Jennings," Mitchell asked, as he and Inson studied the photographs, "how did all those ships disappear in the Bermuda Triangle?"

"Yeah," Inson agreed, " if it wasn't giant squid, what was it?"

"I'll bet I know," Rachel interjected. She was like that. She always thought she knew. "They probably got lost at sea. I read about that. They didn't know where they were going because they had bad compasses."

Mrs. Jennings stopped to explain. "Yes, there may be some truth to that, Rachel. Sailors and ship's captains have reported strange compass readings while they were in the Bermuda Triangle."

"Like the Navy planes from Fort Lauderdale a long time ago!" Mitch chirped. "Their compasses went crazy!"

"Yes, Mitch, that story is quite a mystery, and no trace was ever found."

60

Billy piped in. "Mrs. Jennings, did anyone ever find anything that went missing in the Bermuda Triangle?"

"Well, there's the cargo ship, the Cotopaxi. They've discovered her off the coast of St. Augustine." Mrs. Jennings quickly tapped the keys on her laptop. "Researchers found her all these years later."

Mitch grew very still. His skin was covered with goose pimples. "What?" he said softly "That can't be true...."

"Yes, Mitchell," Mrs. Jennings said, "This is the Cotopaxi," she said as she held up the laptop for all to see. "This ship was missing for nearly 95 years and was considered a victim of the Bermuda Triangle. For nearly a century, her story was a total mystery."

Mitch thought back to Seaman Charles McFarland on the deck of the Cotopaxi, saying,

"Yep, the ol' Cotopaxi. Have you heard that she's a cursed ship?"

"My father says most of the mysteries of the Bermuda Triangle can be explained by science, right, Mrs. Jennings?" Billy chirped.

"Is that true? Can they?" the kids joined in. "Is Billy's father right, Mrs. Jennings?"

Mrs. Jennings hesitated. "Well, I'm no expert, but I do know many of the mysteries have been solved. And we now know that the Cotopaxi didn't really disappear after all."

Mitchell stared off into space. "Didn't really disappear?" he thought to himself. Then he called out, "Where is it? Where is the Cotopaxi now? Seaman Charles said she was taking on water and I ..."

61

Mitch realized that everyone in the classroom was staring at him. "Charles, he–uh– I mean, uh, the Cotopaxi was, um…listing or something…"

"How do you know?" Rachel asked Mitchell. "Do you have some magic power or something?" Rachel was like that. Sarcastic.

"Come on, leave him alone," Jerry chimed in

"Uh, well. I, uh…see, I w–wa–was…" Mitch stammered. "I was talking with my Pop Pop."

"Oh, here we go," Rachel sighed. "It probably has something to do with those binoculars' again. He takes them everywhere."

"Your Pop Pop must have read about the wreck site of the SS Cotopaxi!" Mrs. Jennings said. "The missing Cotopaxi has been one of the most famous Bermuda Triangle disappearances. There was a man who though he knew exactly where the SS Cotopaxi was…and he was right! It turns out the Cotopaxi was hiding under the ocean the whole time. He and other explorers found the Cotopaxi buried under heavy sand, 100 feet below the surface."

Mitch felt a chill go down his spine.

Mrs. Jennings searched her computer. "Ah, here we go." She read: "Marine biologist Michael Barnette teamed up with Guy Walters, a historian, to finally solve the mystery of the missing Cotopaxi. Guy Walters found a previously unknown piece of evidence: the vessel had sent a distress signal that included its position on December 1, 1925. That location was pretty close to a local shipwreck 35 nautical miles off the coast of St. Augustine, Florida, nicknamed "Bear Wreck."

She continued, "Michael Barnette and Guy Walters sought input from the St. Augustine Lighthouse and Maritime Museum and diver Al Perkins to confirm their theory: The Bear Wreck was actually the long–lost SS Cotopaxi."

"What made it sink?" Mitch asked nervously. "Leaky hatch covers?"

Mrs. Jennings searched. "It says here the Cotopaxi sailed into a storm…and evidence showed that the vessel was not seaworthy."

Mitch recalled Seaman Charles telling him:

"Son, the Cotopaxi's hull is tired. She's got a belly full of coal and a gale is in our path. Captain discovered that our ship was riding below the Plimsoll line."

Mrs. Jennings kept reading: "Mr. Michael Barnette, who located the wreck, learned that the ship had sent a radio distress call that helped him determine that it was near St. Augustine before it disappeared.

Michael Barnette

63

"He reported there were several elements that confirmed the identity such as the dimensions of the ship, its length, and the measurement of the boiler."

"It was the hatch covers! The hatches were leaking. Seaman Charles knew that!" Mitch burst out. "The Cotopaxi was taking on water."

"I believe that's correct, Mitchell. You and your Pop Pop surely have studied this." Mrs. Jennings walked back to her desk. "I have an idea. Let's all do more research on the Bermuda Triangle since it's right here off our coast. Let's try to unravel the mystery!"

"Let's try to unravel the mystery!"

8.

CAPTAIN, REPEAT YOUR POSITION.

The dismissal bell rang, and the students scrambled from their desks and headed outside. "Goodbye, Mrs. Jennings," they called in unison.

"Mitch, hey, Mitch." Billy tapped Mitch on his shoulder. "What are you gonna do? Wanna go fishin' down at the river?" The New River was only a short bike ride from the school. "Let's see if we can hook a snapper."

Mitch shook his head as he grabbed his bicycle. "Nah, I want to go home and look up stuff about the Bermuda Triangle. Pop Pop has some good stories about it. Want to come with me instead?" Mitch asked as he climbed onto his old, battered bike.

"More school stuff? Heck no." Billy laughed as he started pedaling away. "I'll be down at the river. Come there if you change your mind."

Mitchell, his mother, and his Pop Pop lived in a small yellow house a few blocks from the school. Mitch raced down the street, tore across the gravel driveway, and dropped his bike in the yard. "Pop Pop!" he called. "Hey, Pop Pop!" Mitch was huffing, trying to catch his breath.

Pop Pop stuck his head out from the kitchen door. "What's with all the noise? It sounds like there's a CAT 4 hurricane out here!" he exclaimed.

"Well, at school today were talking about the Bermuda Triangle," Mitchell panted, "and Mrs. Jennings, she thinks we can solve the mysteries if we study more about it." Mitch sat on a bench in the carport. "So, can you help me, Pop Pop? Will ya? You know a lot about shipwrecks and stuff."

Pop Pop knelt next to Mitch. "Well sure, we can learn some more." Pop Pop led Mitch into the house. "There's so many tales to tell." He paused to look out the kitchen window. I have a story you'll be interested in. A sinking. Happened not all that long ago. A ship was pulled to the bottom in the Bahamas back in 2015. The El Faro."

"Wow!" Mitch chirped. "El Faro! Is that one of the ships that disappeared in the triangle?" Mitch followed Pop Pop into the living room, where his laptop was set up on a large wooden desk. Pop Pop clicked a few keys, and an image filled the screen.

S.S. El Faro

"The S.S. El Faro," he read aloud, "A 790–foot cargo ship with a crew of 33 men. It was the greatest American maritime disaster in 40 years when the ship and her crew disappeared off the coast of the Crooked Island in the Bahamas in 2015."

"Where is Crooked Island?" Mitch asked excitedly. "Is that far from here? Can we take your boat?"

"No, no," Pop Pop replied. "Crooked Island is in the eastern Bahamas, about 400 miles southeast of here."

Chart of the Bahama Islands

"But, but… I thought the Bahamas were closer than that!"

"Yes, some of the Bahamian islands are. The closest island to us is Bimini. It's only about 60 miles offshore," Pop Pop explained.

"Can we see it? If you use your binoculars, can we see Bimini from the beach?" Mitch's mind was doing somersaults. "Can we go to the beach and look for Bimini?"

Pop Pop was always up for a drive. "Sure, Mitch, why don't we bring Austin along? Let's go down to the inlet. You won't be able to see Bimini from there, but there are always ships coming and going."

Mitch and his fuzzy terrier dog, Austin, piled into Pop Pop's car.

"I like to fish from jetty at this inlet," Pop Pop said as his old car rumbled down the road. "Maybe we'll have good luck this time!"

"Can we see Bimini from here? Can we see 60 miles?" Mitch asked as they trudged through the sand. Austin ran on ahead.

"No, that's a bit far. But look what I brought!" Pop Pop reached into a large canvas tote and lifted out the binoculars. "You might even be able to see Crooked Island with these," he laughed. "With a good imagination and a bit of magic! And I brought this." Pop Pop handed Mitch a folded map. "This is a chart of the Bahamas. It might help you with your search." He winked at Mitch as Mitch put the map in his pocket.

Pop Pop walked ahead onto the jetty, while Mitch and Austin stood at the shoreline. The sky was brilliant blue, dotted with wispy clouds. Mitch could see to the horizon.

"Austin, do you think we can see all the way to the Bahamas?"

Austin's tail wagged through the wet sand as Mitch held Pop Pop's binoculars to his eyes. In the distance, he spotted a cargo ship where the sea and sky became one. Mitch tried to focus the binoculars to better see the ship. As he adjusted the focus wheel, the image grew fuzzy. He fiddled with the knob one way, then the other, but the ship would not come into focus. Austin barked loudly.

"What is it, boy?" Mitch called.

The scene in the binoculars grew dark. A cold wind whipped around Mitch as the waves grew higher. "Looks like we'd better get going!" Mitch scanned the shoreline, then searched east for the cargo ship. The focus was now very clear. So clear that Mitch could almost read the name of the vessel. "Capital E something. There's a capital F in the other word...." The wind blew harder, the sea grew angry. As Mitch struggled against the wind, he heard a man's voice.

"We're taking on water! We... starting to list!"

Mitch searched for Pop Pop as the wind pulled at him. "Where is he? Pop Pop!" he called into the storm. "Pop Pop!" Mitch lifted Austin from the blowing sand and held him close to his chest, "What is going on?" They looked for shelter in the leeward side of the jetty, where they would be better protected from the raging wind. "Hey, Pop Pop! Can you hear me?! Where are you?"

Mitch took shelter in the leeward side of the jetty,

Mitch heard the voice again.

"We've got flooding down in the holds," a man yelled. Mitch looked around. There was no one. "Our list is 15 degrees," the man continued. "Does anyone read us?" The wind howled. "We're taking on water and we've lost power."

"Identify your vessel and position," came a crackled reply.

71

"This is the – Cap– of El– ...under control." The message was broken and garbled.

"Captain, repeat your position."

Mitch wiped the salt spray from the binoculars and held them to his eyes. "I'm here!" he yelled into the wind, as he clutched Austin tightly.

"We got...flooding–in three holds...Umm, everybody's safe–not gonna abandon ship...we're gonna stay with the ship...." The voice faded out.

"We need your position," came the crackled response. "Can you read me? What is your last known position?"

"Let me give... latitude and longitude...we're trying – save the ship ...we are forty–eight miles...east of... San Salvador–" The voice broke away in the wind.

"San Salvador?" Mitch thought. He pulled Pop Pop's wet chart from his pocket. The wind was ripping it apart. "Look, Austin. See this? San Salvador is way far out in the ocean! It's closer to Crooked Island than it is to Florida!" The chart broke free from Mitch's hand and flew off in the storm. Mitch tried to focus Pop Pop's binoculars far into the distance. He couldn't see a thing...but he could hear voices from some ship far off in the Atlantic. A ship with an E and an F in its name that was in trouble.

"Bow is down, bow is down! Get into–rafts! Throw all–rafts into the water!" a voice yelled. "Everybody get off! Get off ... stay together!"

"We're taking on water! We... we're starting to list!"

Mitch felt someone tousling his wind–swept hair.

"Ready to go, Mitch? I guess I should have checked the weather report before we left," Pop Pop laughed. He was soaking wet. "That storm came up suddenly!"

Mitch jolted in surprise. "Pop Pop?! Oh, Pop Pop! I've been looking for you!" Mitch lowered Austin to the ground. "Where were you?" He gave Pop Pop a wet bear–hug.

"Heh, heh… I was looking for you, too! You were smart to find a bit of shelter here by the jetty." Pop Pop looked into Austin's eyes. "You, my friend, look like a drowned rat!" he chuckled.

"Pop Pop, did you hear? Did you hear the calls for help?" Mitch asked excitedly.

"What calls? From where?" Pop Pop said as he looked all around the jetties. "Was someone in trouble?"

"A ship, Pop Pop, a ship is in trouble! Taking on water!"

"Where?"

"Near San Salvador! I looked on the chart, then it blew away in the wind." Mitch explained. "They're abandoning ship! I heard them."

Pop Pop cocked his head to one side and gave Mitch an inquisitive stare. "A ship near San Salvador. You heard calls for help from a ship near San Salvador? Hundreds of miles away? Does this ship have a name?"

"I know there's a capital letter E and a capital letter F–I saw it!"

"You saw the ship? You even saw part of the ship's name?" Pop Pop laughed. "I think that imagination of yours got the best of you!"

"Through these!" Mitch chirped as he held up Pop Pop's binoculars. They were crusty with sand and salt spray. "I saw the ship through these!" Mitch handed the binoculars to Pop Pop. "And I could hear the captain!"

74

Pop Pop knelt next to Mitch. He scratched Austin's wet, shaggy ears. "I think our talk about the sinking of the El Faro was on your mind. And maybe this storm played tricks on you. Sometimes the wind coming in from the ocean can sound just like voices." He brushed sand off the black binoculars. "The lenses are pretty smudged. You may have seen something out there, but it wasn't El Faro. She went down years ago…she's in the Bahamas, sitting upright on the bottom of the Atlantic. "

He winked at Mitch and examined the binoculars. "Imagination sure can be a powerful thing," he said. "Yep, a powerful thing."

"Imagination sure can be a powerful thing."

Pop Pop slipped the binoculars into their leather case and placed it around Mitch's neck. The late afternoon setting sun was peeking out from behind a thick cluster of coconut palms. "Let's go home, Mitchell. Your mother will wonder what's keeping us." Mitch and Pop Pop trudged through the sand while Austin ran ahead, his pink tongue dangling from the side of his mouth. "So, do you think you have enough for your school project now?" Pop Pop asked.

"Yeah. I think so…" Mitch replied. "But I'm not sure the kids are going to believe me. I'm not so sure I believe me, either!"

9.

SOME OF THE MOST FAMOUS MYSTERIES
OF THE BERMUDA TRIANGLE

The US Navy estimates that approximately 50 ships and 20 aircraft have disappeared in the Bermuda Triangle, which is also known as the 'Devil's Triangle,' the 'Hoodoo Sea,' and the 'Limbo of the Lost." The triangle, which makes up an area of roughly a half a million square miles in the Atlantic Ocean, has a long history of mystery.

Christopher Columbus

In a journal belonging to Christopher Columbus from the 1400s, the explorer mentioned that his ship's compass went berserk as the ship entered "an unseen boundary" between Florida and Puerto Rico. It took several weeks for Columbus and his crew to make the trip that should have taken far less time. During this voyage, he wrote that he saw "a great flame of fire" fall into the sea. Perhaps Columbus saw a meteor falling into the ocean.

Columbus, and many sailors through the centuries after him, found themselves in an area of water that caused their ships to become trapped, entangled in endless seaweed. Lost and abandoned ships are legendary in this area of the Atlantic Ocean between Bermuda and the Bahamas now referred to as the Sargasso Sea. The calm waters and thick seaweed could be deadly to ships under sail that were unable to break free. Today's powerful boats and ships are far less affected by the currents.

William Shakespeare

Some scholars theorize that the play, "The Tempest" by William Shakespeare, may have been based on a Bermuda shipwreck. The opening scene of The Tempest takes place aboard a ship being torn and tossed by a horrific storm. The ship is splintered into ruins.

Many scholars and researchers believe a real shipwreck, the Sea Venture, off Bermuda in 1609, was William Shakespeare's inspiration for this scene. "The Tempest" is believed to have been written in 1610–11 and is thought to be the last play written by William Shakespeare.

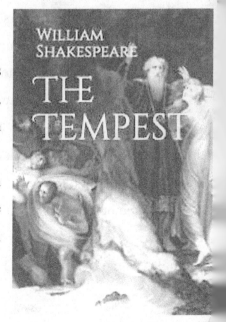

Marie Celeste

On December 5, 1872, the Marie Celeste sailed from New York Harbor loaded with cargo, but she never made it to her destination. Eventually, she was found drifting with her sails up in the Bermuda Triangle. Her crew and captain were missing.

All her cargo and lifeboats were aboard, but oddly there was rotting food left behind on plates in her galley. The reason the crew left a ship that appeared to be seaworthy has never been explained.

Joshua Slocum and "Spray"

In 1895, the first man to sail solo around the world, Joshua Slocum, vanished on a voyage from Martha's Vineyard to South America aboard his sailboat, Spray. It was odd that Slocum had been lost at sea, given his extensive sailing experience. His disappearance was later attributed to the Bermuda Triangle.

The U.S.S. Cyclops

On February 16, 1918, the Cyclops left Rio de Janeiro and headed for Baltimore, Maryland. She was heavily loaded with 11,000 tons of manganese ore, which would have been used to create munitions in the United States during World War 1. Before leaving Rio de Janeiro, her crew reported that the starboard engine was not running. There were no stops planned, but Cyclops did make a stop in Barbados because she was overloaded. After being cleared, Cyclops headed for Baltimore on March 4, 1918 – but never reached her destination. Cyclops and her crew of 306 men seemingly disappeared. There were no SOS distress calls and no remains of the ship were found. The US Navy declared that the ship was lost, and all crew had perished. A news reporter at the time thought it was possible the ship was the target of German U–boats. No one aboard had responded to any of the hundreds of radio calls made from American ships.

COLLIER CYCLOPS WITH 293 ABOARD IS LONG OVERDUE

Big Naval Vessel Last Reported at West Indies Island March 4; All Efforts of Department to Solve Mystery of Her Disappearance Unsuccessful; Anxiety Felt for Safety.

A magazine writer suggested that a giant octopus had risen from the sea, entwined the ship with its tentacles, and dragged it to the bottom. Other rumors stated that Commander Worley had locked up the crew and delivered Cyclops to their war enemy.

It's generally accepted that Cyclops didn't disappear, and she didn't fall prey to giant octopus or a U–boat attack. She likely sank because she was dangerously overloaded and was underpowered due to a broken engine. Researchers found that a ship her size, which was badly overloaded, would not be able to ride the peaks and swells of an Atlantic squall for long. In former president Woodrow Wilson's words, "Only God and the sea know what happened to the great ship." Oddly, years later, one of the Cyclops' sister ships, USS Proetus, vanished in the same area while carrying a cargo of bauxite ore, used to make aluminum. She disappeared without a trace in November 1941.

Of the 300 sailors aboard the U.S.S. Cyclops, only four of her crew were African–American. Earl Whitehall was one of them. He came from Colorado to serve aboard the U.S.S. Cyclops as a fireman. Andrew Theodore Askin of Pennsylvania, Lewis Hardwick and Survian Austin Williams of D.C. worked in the galley and mess hall. At the time, the African American sailors were segregated from the rest of the crew and had to sleep and eat in separate areas.

The US Navy would be fully integrated until July 1948, by order of President Truman, although practices of discrimination continued.

ANDREW THEODORE ASKIN.
Mess Attendant 3c, U. S. N.
Lost on U. S. S. CYCLOPS, June 14, 1918.

LEWIS H. HARDWICK.
Mess Attendant, 3c, U. S. N.
Lost on U. S. S. CYCLOPS, June 14, 1918.

EARLE B. WHITESELL.
Fireman, 3c, U. S. N.
Lost on U. S. S. CYCLOPS, June 14, 1918.

SURVIAN AUSTIN WILLIAMS.
Mess Attendant U. S. N.
Lost on U. S. S. CYCLOPS, June 14, 1918.

Flight 19 and Rescue Efforts

At 2:10 p.m. on December 5, 1945, five TBM Avenger torpedo bombers took off from the Naval Air Station, NASFTL, for a training flight from Fort Lauderdale, Florida. The group of planes was referred to as Flight 19. By 6.00 p.m. that evening, radio contact with the pilots was lost. None of the planes nor their 14 Navy crewmen were ever seen or heard from again.

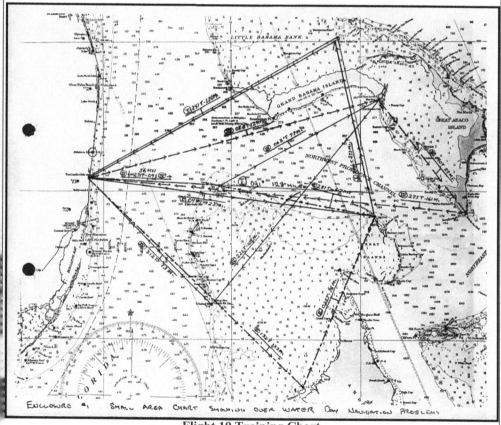

Flight 19 Training Chart

Just minutes after the radios of Flight 19 went silent, the Navy began searching for the missing planes. Two PBM Mariners, categorized as flying boats, were sent from the Naval Air Station, Banana River near Cocoa Beach, Florida (now Patrick Space Force Base). They flew a grid pattern of the area west of Flight 19's last calculated position, 29°N 79°W. Twenty minutes after take-off, one of the Mariner flying boats vanished from the radar screens. There was no distress call. No trace of the lost PBM Mariner nor her 13 crewmen were ever discovered.

PBM Mariner 'Flying Boats'

The US Navy dispatched more than 300 boats and aircraft to search for clues from Flight 19 and the missing PBM Mariner. The search lasted more than five days and covered an area of more than 300,000 square miles. Nothing was ever found.

In the decades since, it is accepted that the 5 Avenger planes that comprised Flight 19 ran out of gas as they searched for landmarks. They likely ditched in the ocean off the coast of Florida. If any of the airmen survived the impact of hitting the water at a high rate of speed, they would have faced rough seas, deep water and perhaps sharks.

A merchant ship cited a fireball and spotted an oil slick in the ocean in the area where the PBM Mariner vanished. It is believed the Mariner caught fire and exploded shortly after takeoff.

After WWII, many PMB Mariner Flying Boats had been modified to fit larger fuel tanks for long-range flights. The Navy soon reported a very high rate of accidents due to this change and Navy airmen referred to the Mariners as "flying gas tanks" because they often caught fire in flight.

It is possible that Flight 19 and the Mariner are hiding under the Atlantic Ocean, somewhere in the Bermuda Triangle, but no remains of any of the aircraft or the 27 crewmen from the two missions have been found.

Oddly, in 1989, a laywer named Graham Stikelether was hunting in a Florida swamp and came upon wreckage of an TBM

Avenger. Mr. Stikelether knew the wreckage was old, but could find no identifying marks. Had this plane been part of Flight 19?

Deeping the mystery about the Avenger wreck is a telegram which had been received on December 26, 1945, just 21 days after his Flight 19 vanished. The telegram seemed to indicate that Staff Sergeant George Paonessa, who was the radioman aboard Flight 19 TBM Avenger FT – 36, had actually survived. It was sent to Sergeant Paonessa's brother, Joseph, in Jacksonville, Florida and read, "You have been misinformed about me. Am very much alive. Georgie."

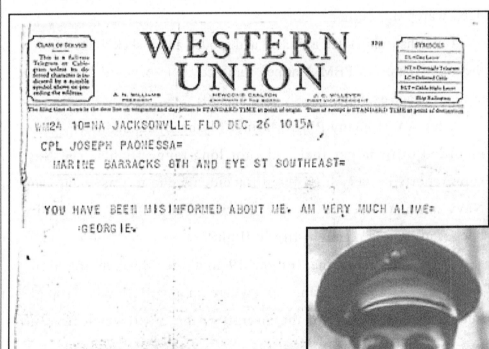

Staff Sergeant George Paonessa

Had FT-36 made it to land? Did Sergeant Paonessa make it out of the plane before it crashed into the Florida swampland? At that point, the identity of the plane discovered in 1989 was unsolved. Whether the telegram was actually real is unknown.

But was this TBM Avenger wreckage actually from FT-36?

A rubber heel found at the wreckage site came from a size 11 or 12 shoe, a close match to shoes worn by Flight 19 Leader, Lieutenant Taylor aboard FT-28. The Navy had not reported a TBM Avenger missing anywhere in Florida between 1944 and 1952, therefore researchers believed the Everglades wreck did belong to Flight 19.

But by 2014, after a thorough review of Navy records, it was determined the plane found had been flown by Ensign Ralph N. Wachob from the Naval Air Station in Miami. Ensign Wachob crashed in the swamps of western Broward County and was killed on March 16, 1947, nearly a year and half months Flight 19 disappeared.

Wachob was on a navigational training flight from Miami to Tampa with two other planes. He reported losing sight of his flight leader, became lost, disoriented and crashed. A day after the accident, Navy officials investigated the accident and left the wreckage deep in the remote Everglades. The Navy Accident Report clarified that the he TBM-3 Avenger's pilot was Ralph Wachob, not Charles Taylor. Wachob was the only one aboard.

In May 1989, 42 years after Ensign Wachob's Avenger crashed, the wreckage left behind by the Navy was rediscovered after an

Everglades brush fire burned down the tall sawgrass that had kept it well hidden.

Flight 19 Squadron, all presumed lost:

FT – 28
- Flight Leader: Lt. Charles Carroll Taylor, USNR.
- Aircraft: TBM–3D
  Gunner: George Francis Devlin,
- Radioman: Walter Reed Parpart, Jr.

FT – 36
- Pilot: Capt. Earl Joseph Powers, USMC.
- Aircraft: TBM–1C
- Gunner: Sgt. Howell Orrin Thompson, USMCR.
- Radioman: Sgt. George Richard Paonessa, USMCR.

FT – 81
- Pilot: 2nd Lt. Forrest James Gerber, USMCR.
- Aircraft: TBM–1C
- Crew: Pfc. William Lightfoot, USMCR.

FT– 3
- Pilot: Ensign Joseph Tipton Bossi, USNR.
- Aircraft: TBM–1C
- Gunner: Herman Arthur Thelander, USNR.
- Radioman: Burt E. Baluk, USNR.

FT– 117

- Pilot: Captain George William Stivers Jr., USMC.

- Aircraft: TBM–1C

- Crew: Gunner USMCR

- Radioman: Pvt. Robert Peter Gruebel,

- Gunner Sgt. Robert Francis Gallivan, USMCR

- Radioman: Pvt. Robert Peter Gruebel, USMCR

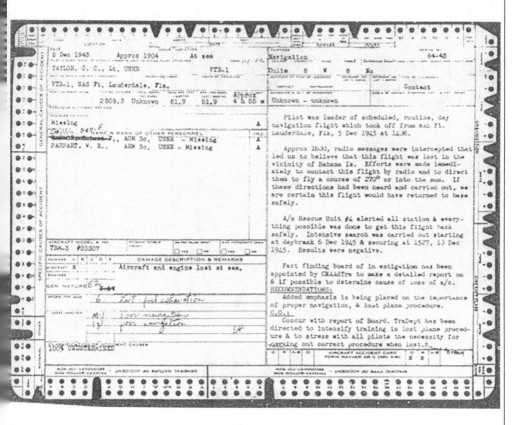

THE SQUADRON

TBM AVENGERS

FT - 28

FT - 36

FT - 81

FT - 3

FT - 117

Lt. Charles C. Taylor
Flight Leader on FT-28

George F. Devlin
MMMc, USNR Gunner on FT-28

Howell Orvin Thompson
Sgt., USMC - Gunner on FT-36

Capt. Edward J. Powers
USMC - pilot on FT-36

Capt. George William Stivers, Jr.
USMC - pilot on FT-117

Ensign Joseph Tipton Bossi
USNR - pilot on FT-3

Robert P. Gruebel
Pvt. USMCR on FT-117

William Earl Lightfoot
Pfc, USMCR on FT-81

Robert F. Gallivan
Sgt.USMC on FT-117

Herman A. Thelander
S1c, USNR - Gunner on FT-3

George R. Paonessa
Sgt. USMC-Radioman on FT-3

Burt Edward Baluk, Jr.
S1c, USNR Radioman on FT-3

2nd Lt. Forrest J. Gerber
USMCR on FT-81

Left to right: Edward Baluk from Flight 19; Lt. Robert F. Cox, USNR Senior Flight Instructor, who was out and talking with the Flight 19 crew until their signal got weaker and George Devlin from Flight 19, circa 1945.

Flight 19 - The Lost Squadron

On December 5, 1945, a Squadron of 5 TBM Avenger airplanes with 14 men from the Naval Air Station Fort Lauderdale vanished in the Bermuda Triangle. A massive search and rescue ensued. 13 other men aboard a PBM Mariner from the rescue mission also disappeared. No trace was ever found. Flight 19 remains one of the great aviation mysteries.

Other Wartime Planes

During World War II many war planes flew over the Atlantic to assist the British and Americans. A few of them disappeared without a trace over the Bermuda Triangle, including the British South American Airways 'Star Tiger', the British South American Airways 'Star Ariel' and a 'Douglas DC–3' flown by the British Royal Air Force.

On December 28, 1948, a DC–3 passenger plane took off at dawn, flying from San Juan, Puerto Rico to Miami, Florida, a distance of about 1,000 miles. The plane's captain radioed the control tower in Miami stating that the passengers and crew were singing Christmas carols. A few hours later, the captain radioed again to say the plane was approaching the airport.

Before departure, the pilot had told the airline's repair crew that the landing gear warning light was not working and the plane's batteries were very weak, but he did not delay the flight.

Air traffic controllers in Miami heard radio transmissions from a New Orleans airport that the flight was 50 miles south of Miami. The call, made by the plane's captain, reported that the plane would soon be approaching the airport at Miami. It was the last communication heard from the DC–3 passenger plane.

A search was made by dozens of aircraft and ships from the Coast Guard, Air Force, and Navy, but no trace of the flight, its crew or passengers was ever discovered.

DC–3 passenger plane

Just weeks later, on January 17, 1949, a Tudor IV aircraft departed Bermuda for Jamaica with 7 crew members and 13 passengers. The captain reported that the flight was going well, but a later message from the captain stated he was changing radio frequencies. He did not explain the reason. The plane was never heard from again. A search turned up no debris or wreckage.

A year earlier, on January 30, 1948, a British South American Airways Tudor IV plane flying from England to Bermuda disappeared without a trace. The captain had reported he expected to arrive on schedule, yet neither he nor any of the 32 people onboard the flight were ever heard from again.

Reports uncovered that the plane's heater was known to be faulty. It is thought that, to keep the passengers warm, the pilot had been flying at a low altitude. Flying low could have affected the pilot's ability to maneuver properly. The flight may have lost altitude and fallen into the Atlantic Ocean.

S.S. Marine Sulphur Queen

The tanker, S.S. Marine Sulphur Queen, disappeared off the southern coast of Florida in February 1963 while carrying a load of molten sulfur. There was no trace of wreckage or any of the 39 crewmen. A US Coast Guard investigation revealed the ship may not have been seaworthy.

S.S. Marine Sulphur Queen

S.S. Marine Sulphur Queen

The Marine Sulphur Queen had a design flaw, known as a "weak back." This flaw could have caused the keel to split if it had been weakened by corrosion. Additionally, the ship had been converted to carry a heavy load of molten sulfur. The shifting weight of this cargo may have rendered the ship more vulnerable to capsize. The sinking of SS Marine Sulphur Queen was considered to be a result of her poor condition rather than a mystery.

The U.S.S. Scorpion

The United States Navy submarine 'Scorpion' carried Navy secret spy equipment, two nuclear torpedoes and 99 crewmen. Scorpion was very advanced for its time, propelled by nuclear power.

Scorpion departed from the Mediterranean Sea just after midnight on Friday, May 17, 1968, and was expected to arrive in Norfolk, Virginia on May 27. When Scorpion did not arrive, Navy officials became concerned. Soon, aircraft from Norfolk and Bermuda began to search for any sign of the missing submarine. In late October 1968, the US Navy reported that the wreckage of the submarine had been found. Navy surveillance hydrophones in the Atlantic had detected an explosion and a Russian submarine was tracked leaving the area at a high rate of speed. All aboard were "presumed lost."

Crew members aboard U.S.S. Scorpion

Image of the stern section of the wreck of U.S.S. Scorpion

The NASA Space Shuttle Challenger

While a documentary about U.S. Navy Air Flight 19 was being filmed in 2022, a team discovered a huge piece of the 1986 Space Shuttle Challenger on the floor of the Atlantic Ocean near the Bermuda Triangle.

On January 28, 1986, Challenger exploded 73 seconds into its flight. The crew died when the shuttle broke apart 46,000 feet above the ocean off the coast of Florida. Until this section was discovered, it was believed that all pieces of the Challenger had previously been recovered.

The S.S. El Faro

A more recent tragedy was the loss of The S.S. El Faro in 2015. El Faro left Jacksonville, Florida, and headed for Puerto Rico on September 29, 2015. Quickly her crew found themselves in the path of Joaquin, a Category 4 hurricane. Winds approached 130 mph and seas reached 40 feet. At 7:30 a.m. on October 1, helmsman Frank Hamm, reported that El Faro was taking on a great deal of water and was listing (leaning) 15 degrees. Her cargo had broken loose and was crashing about inside her hull. The captain, Michael Davidson, radioed that the flooding was under control... then communication with SS El Faro was lost.

On October 31, 2015, after extensive searching, Navy ship USNS Apache located the wreckage of El Faro. She was found intact, sitting upright on her keel. No trace of her 33 crew members was ever found. Was S.S. El Faro's sinking a mystery? Not likely. Former crew members stated that the ship was "a rust bucket", that her decks were full of holes, and she should have never been near water. She didn't have proper safety equipment and there was no anemometer aboard to measure the speed of the wind as she entered Hurricane Joaquin in the Caribbean Sea.

S.S. El Faro

These are actual transcripts from radio calls received from S.S. El Faro:

<u>09/13/2105 – 6:57</u>

"It's miserable right now. ...a scuttle was left open or popped open or whatever, so we got some flooding down in three holds—a significant amount. Umm, everybody's safe right now, we're not gonna abandon ship—we're gonna stay with the ship"!

<u>09/13/2105–7:06</u>

"I have a marine emergency and I would like to speak with a Qualified Individual. We had a hull breach– a scuttle blew open during the storm. We have water down in three holds. We have a heavy list. We've lost the main propulsion unit. The engineers cannot get it goin'."

"We have uhh secured the source of water coming into the vessel. Uh, A scuttle was blown open ... it's since been closed. However, uh, three holds got a considerable amount of water in it. Uh, we have a very, very healthy port list. The engineers cannot get lube oil pressure on the plant, therefore we've got no main engine, and let me give you, um, a latitude and longitude. The crew is safe. Right now we're trying to save the ship now, – We are forty–eight miles east of San Salvador.

"We are taking every measure to… pump out that– pump out that hold the best we can– Our safest bet is to stay with the ship during this particular time. The weather is ferocious out here and we're gonna stay with the ship."

"We still got reserve buoyancy and stability." Captain Davidson then gave the order to abandon ship, and about a minute later, could be heard calling out, "Bow is down, bow is down! Get into your rafts! Throw all your rafts into the water! Everybody get off! Get off the ship! Stay together!"

The radio transmission ends at 7:39 a.m., with the captain and helmsman still aboard. Although the El Faro was a victim of poor maintenance and a terrible storm, her story has helped keep the mystery of the Bermuda Triangle alive.

Wreck of the S.S. El Faro resting on the bottom. All aboard were lost.

10.

WHAT MIGHT EXPLAIN THE DISAPPEARANCES IN THE BERMUDA TRIANGLE?

Storms and Magnetic Oddities

The National Oceanic and Atmospheric Administration (NOAA) feels that these oddities can be explained. NOAA has found evidence which suggests the Bermuda Triangle holds a geomagnetic feature that could cause a compass to point to "true" north rather than "magnetic" north. This could cause navigation systems in ships and planes to function improperly. Magnetic north is tied to the metal in the Earth's core, which tilts and shifts with the planet. True north is tied to the actual North Pole of the planet.

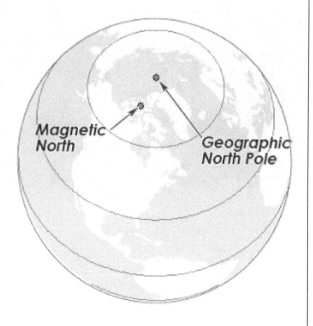

NOAA further explains that the Bermuda Triangle is home to dozens of strong storms and hurricanes each year, as well as the Gulf Stream current, which can generate significant and rapid changes in the weather.

Giant Methane Gas Bubbles

Theories have been 'floated' (pardon the pun) about nature's release of methane gas from the ocean floor that could bubble to the surface and cause a ship to sink. Large methane bubbles disrupt the density of the sea water as well as the surface tension. Ships are designed to float on the water's surface at specific densities. The surface density of the Atlantic Ocean is approximately 64lbs. per cubic foot (1 foot wide, 1 foot deep, 1 foot across). Giant bubbles of methane gas from the ocean floor may reduce the surface tension, but scientists and researchers agree that even the largest methane gas bubble would not cause a ship to sink.

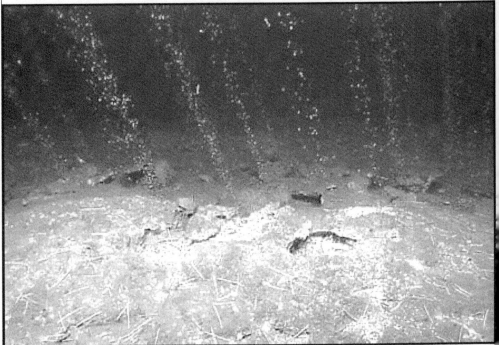

Methane gas from the ocean floor

Rogue Waves

Rogue waves are abnormally large waves that may develop when storm systems collide. The winds from two or more storms cause waves to combine from different directions. These combined wave crests can then produce a giant rogue wave, which can potentially reach 100 feet.

The Gulf Stream, which runs through the Bermuda Triangle, is a fast–moving current that can create rogue waves under the right conditions. Waves in the Gulf Stream bend, swirl and come together, creating taller and taller waves. Scientists have learned that areas of the Bermuda Triangle are prone to rogue waves.

The Lost City of Atlantis

Could the Bermuda Triangle hold the secrets from the mythical Lost City of Atlantis? According to legend, Atlantis was created by Poseidon, the Greek God of the Seas. It is told that Atlantis was destroyed and sunk into the deepest trenches of the Atlantic Ocean because of the sinful behavior of its inhabitants. Legend says that underwater creatures holding Atlantean fire–crystals still hold power over the ocean above the lost city.

Artist's concept of the Lost City of Atlantis

Aliens

There are some theorists who believe that UFOs caused the mysterious disappearances in the Bermuda Triangle. Some of these theories propose that the Bermuda Triangle is a gathering station where aliens capture humans from ships and aircraft. The area serves as a portal for aliens to travel to and from Earth.

Undersea Monsters

Sea monsters have existed in folklore for centuries and are believed to live deep in every ocean and sea on our planet. These creatures are imagined to take the form of huge sea dragons, sea serpents, or giant squid and octopus with immense tentacles.

Even Christopher Columbus believed in mythical sea creatures. While sailing off the coast of Haiti, he saw what he thought were mermaids. They were most likely manatees.

It is possible that the myths surrounding these creatures were created because of concern for ships that disappeared during storms and for the sailors that never came back home. It was likely easier to imagine that a creature of some sort was responsible for their disappearance—especially since many sea monster stories leave room for the victims to be alive and well somewhere. Legends tell of giant sea creatures who kidnap humans and force them to remain under the surface of the sea for the rest of their lives.

Seaweed. Yes, Seaweed!

Spinning in the cold water of the Atlantic Ocean lies the Sargasso Sea. The water in the Sargasso Sea is much warmer and filled with thick clumps of Sargasso seaweed. In 1840, the unfortunate vessel Rosalie found its way into the Sargasso Sea and could not escape the seaweed. Later that same year, she was discovered floating adrift with her sails up, but no crew aboard.

Throughout the 1800s, the area was thought to hold mystical powers, which would capture ships for eternity, not allowing their crews to escape.

Several ships were found drifting in circles, caught in the strong current and a tangle of seaweed. Tales were told of sailing ships being

devoured by monstrous weeds. The Sargasso Sea was featured in books by Jules Verne, among other authors from the 1800s.

The mystery of the Sargasso Sea isn't really much of a mystery. The strong, circular current simply old wind–powered sailing ships powerless, creating the legend.

Earthquakes and Tsunamis

The surface of the Earth is divided into 7 major and 8 minor plates. These plates are in always in motion and they rub against one another along their edges, known as 'plate boundaries'. The friction from this rubbing can create volcanoes and earthquakes.

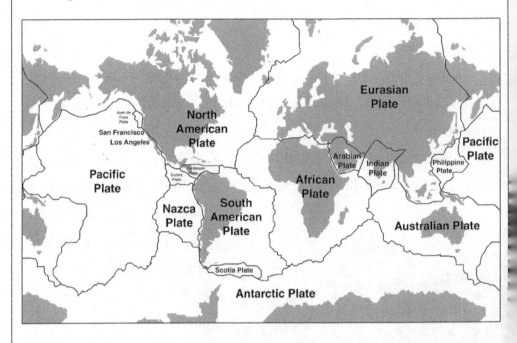

The island of Puerto Rico, which creates the southern point of the Bermuda Triangle, sits between the North American plate and a northeast corner of the Caribbean plate. The North American Plate is situated along the Puerto Rico Trench, the deepest water in the southern Atlantic Ocean, nearly 2.2 miles deep.

The island of Puerto Rico and the seafloor that surrounds it can get squeezed between these two plates. When enough force is created, earthquakes can occur, as happened in this area of the Caribbean Sea in 1918, 1943, 1946 and 1953.

Once an earthquake occurs, the floor of the ocean begins to shake quickly, which forces large amounts of water to thrust outward in different directions. As this water builds in volume and speed, a tsunami is formed.

In 1946, a tsunamis killed more than 1800 people in Puerto Rico and Hispaniola. A 1918 tsunami killed at least 40 people in Puerto Rico and an 1867 tsunami created 23-foot waves that tossed a large naval ship on top of a pier.

The presence of earthquakes and the resulting tsunamis in the Bermuda Triangle could easily explain the disappearance of ships and vessels throughout the centuries.

Underwater Sink Holes and Whirlpools

Approximately 30 miles southeast of the city of Saint Augustine lies Red Snapper Sink, a huge underwater sinkhole. The opening is 400 feet across and 100 feet beneath the surface on the floor of the Atlantic Ocean. At 150 feet down, the opening narrows, forming a funnel-like shape and remains narrow all the way to the bottom of the hole itself, a more than 600 feet below the floor of the ocean.

Off the east coast of Florida and throughout the Caribbean Sea there exists a network of very deep underwater holes, caverns and pits connected by underground passageways. They are believed to have been dry caves and caverns that filled with water when sea levels rose after the Ice Age, approximately 8,000-14,000 years ago.

Because of the incredible depth, the water at the surface of a hole is dark blue, far darker than the water that surrounds them. These openings have been nicknamed blue holes. **One example is Dean's Blue Hole in the Bahamas, the second deepest underwater sinkhole in the world, with a depth 663 feet.** It is estimated that 1,000 blue holes exist in the Bahamas, but only a few have been explored.

But do these sinkholes under the ocean floor create huge, powerful whirlpools that can sink a ship like the S.S. Cyclops? Although whirlpool wave action has been documented in the Bermuda Triangle, and other areas of the Atlantic Ocean, the waves patterns often result from a combination of forces from the changing tides and the currents of the Gulf Stream.

111

Red Snapper Sink has been thoroughly explored by deep sea divers and no wreckage of any ship was discovered. Divers have also explored the depths of Dean's Blue Hole and no wreckage was found there, either. There are no accounts of any ship being drawn into a whirlpool and forced into a sinkhole, hundreds of feet below the sea floor.

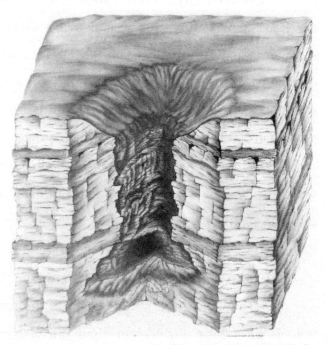

Dean's Blue Hole

Profile of Red Snapper Sink

Can All the Mysteries of the Bermuda Triangle be Explained?

The mystery of the Bermuda Triangle may not be a mystery at all. The US Navy and US Coast Guard have found no evidence to support the idea of any "supernatural" events that caused disasters and disappearances. Their experience suggests that nature's storms and human mistakes can explain the majority of incidents.

There is no official map that marks the boundaries of the Bermuda Triangle. The U. S. Navy does not recognize the Bermuda Triangle as an official name. This triangle makes up a large area of the western Atlantic Ocean, but it is not on any officially recognized printed map.

Travel on or over the Atlantic Ocean has always been dangerous – and mysterious. Storms and hurricanes, strong air and water currents, and human navigation errors can result in tragedy. In the storm–tossed waters of the Atlantic, there is never a guarantee of safety.

There is no evidence that ships and planes disappear more often in the Bermuda Triangle than in any other large, well–traveled area of ocean. The deep waters of the Bermuda Triangle (between 3.5 miles to 5 miles deep in the Puerto Rico Trench) and the powerful currents of the Gulf Stream, which moves the wreckage and debris, can make locating missing ships and planes nearly impossible.

There will always be those who believe the triangle holds unexplained mysteries, and there are others who believe there are basic reasons for the unusual circumstances…but there is no doubt that the Bermuda Triangle will always be a source of good storytelling!

Made in the USA
Columbia, SC
13 November 2023

26115607R00065